This **Picture Mammoth** belongs to

Shea Carson
_____

FEBUARY 04,05
_____

♡ DADDY + Kyle

Tyler XOXOX.

First day home.

Learning to crawl.

At the seaside.

First steps.

Eating by myself...

... is good fun.

All gone!

Music time.

First birthday.

For Claire

When I was a Baby

Catherine Anholt

"What's that?"
"It's a baby vest."
"Was that my vest?"
"Yes, just think how small
  you must have been."

"When we brought you back from
   the hospital wrapped in a woolly shawl,
   you were no bigger than a doll."

"What did I eat when I was a baby?"
"For a long time you only drank milk."
"Didn't I eat apples?"
"No, because at first you didn't have any teeth."

"Is that me, sleeping in that little basket?"
"Yes. Lots of people came to see you and
sometimes they brought you presents."

"Daddy used to bath you in that
  red plastic bath, just like you bath your doll."
"Did I splash him?"
"Yes, you've always loved playing in the water."

"When I was a baby I wore nappies, didn't I?"
"Yes. When they were wet you used to cry
  and we would put a dry one on."
"Did I stop crying then?"
"Yes. Then you went back to sleep again."

"My doll likes going for a walk in the park."
"Yes. Once you used to like riding in a pram.
  We used to push you everywhere."

"As you grew bigger, you had a highchair, too,
so that you could sit at the table with us."
"Did I make a mess when I ate my dinner?"
"Yes, but you soon learned to feed yourself."

"Was I a noisy baby?"
"You certainly were.
  Once you could sit up, your favourite game was
  banging a saucepan with a wooden spoon."

"I remember one day you
  got lost in the garden.
  You cried and cried.
  You'd crawled right off
  the grass into the flower bed."
"And then you came and found me!"

"Did I have a party when I was a baby?"
"You did when you were one.
  All your friends came to tea
  and I made you a special birthday cake."

"I'm not one now!"
"No. Now you're three."
"I'm not a baby any more.
  Now I'm three, I'm big."

First day home.

Learning to crawl.

At the seaside.

First steps.

Eating by myself...

... is good fun.

All gone!

Music time.

First birthday.

First published in Great Britain 1988
by William Heinemann Ltd
Published 1990 by Mammoth
an imprint of Reed International Books Ltd.
Michelin House, 81 Fulham Road, London SW3 6RB

10 9 8 7 6 5 4 3

Copyright © Catherine Anholt 1988

ISBN 0 7497 0316 4

A CIP catalogue record for this title is available from the British Library

Printed in the U.A.E. by Oriental Press Ltd.